A SLOTH LIKE LOVE

SHIFTERS UNLIMITED #4

STEVIE SHIMMERCOX

SURRENDERED PRESS

Surrendered Press

A Sloth Like Love

Copyright © 2021 by Stevie Shimmercox

All rights reserved.

CONTENTS

ONE

BRANDON

"You're late," Pop called over his shoulder.

"I know, I'm sorry," I panted, throwing my jacket over the hook. "I'll stay late to make up for it." The welcoming aroma of melted cheese and roasted meat and vegetables wrapped around me like a cozy blanket.

"Pah! You have better things to do on a Friday night than working." Pop waved me off. He wasn't my father, but he certainly treated me like family. My own dad had died years ago, my mom years before that, and as soon as Pop found out that I was an orphan, it became almost a personal mission of his to make me feel at home here.

I wrapped the half-apron around my waist and tucked in a pad of paper and a pen, then I rushed out toward the dining room. It was quiet, we hadn't hit the dinner rush yet, but in an hour, this place would be packed. Fat Pizza was the best pizza place in the city, and everybody knew it.

David saw me coming and gave a wave. "There you are. Pop was starting to get worried."

"I was two minutes late," I said with a laugh.

"Yeah, but you know Pop."

"I do. Any tables for me?"

"Yeah, just the guy over by the window. He's been looking at that menu for like twenty minutes." David rolled his eyes. "He's probably just here for the free breadsticks and drink refills."

I looked over at the customer, and my heart gave a little staccato beat in my chest. "Damn," I whispered.

"Tell me about it," David agreed with a nod. "If I weren't already taken, I would be all over that man."

He was tall and lean, obviously well-muscled under that button-up shirt of his. His dark hair was slicked back, and his jaw was grazed with a light beard. He was all kinds of fine. Just the shape of him made me slick.

As if he knew we were talking about him, his piercing eyes darted up and met mine. He promptly folded his menu up and set it to the side, giving me a chin nod to indicate he was ready to order.

"There you go," David said, giving me a nudge with his elbow. "You're welcome."

I tried to laugh, but it got caught in my throat and came out as more of a sputter. I could feel the blush warming my cheeks as I headed over to the table. My throat dried up, and I had to clear my throat three times before I could ask, "Hi... I mean, what can I get you this evening? Or is it afternoon?" Gods, throw a hot alpha at me and I turned into a blubbering idiot.

He licked his lips, and my eyes couldn't help but follow his tongue's path. Would it be wrong of me to drink his water? Maybe dump the entire thing over my head? I was getting seriously warm right now. It was a good thing I had an apron across my crotch, or he would be getting an eyeful.

"Are you Brandon?" he asked. His voice was deep and smooth, and I was so enthralled by its timber that it took me a moment to register his words. Not a food order.

I tapped my name tag, which clearly said Brandon. "Yep. And I will be your server for today." Any kind of service, not restricted to what was on the menu.

"Brandon Mills?" he elaborated.

I narrowed my eyes. My name tag didn't have my last name.

And then he lowered his voice and cast a furtive look around the dining room. "The sloth shifter, Brandon Mills?"

The heat I had been feeling was suddenly gone, and it was like I was plunged into an ice bath. Goose-bumps raised across my skin. I breathed deeply, testing the man's scent, but he was clearly human. What was a human alpha doing looking for me, and why did he know I was a shifter?

"Who's asking?" An uneasy anxiety began to creep up from my toes.

He held out his hand to shake. "William Knowles. I'm a recruiter for Shifters Unlimited." As if that clarified anything. I let his proffered hand hover there for a moment. It seemed innocuous enough. We were in a public place, after all.

I wrapped my hand around his, and it sent an electric shot straight down to my crotch.

He seemed reluctant to let go but finally released his grip and indicated with his hand to the chair across from him. "Please, sit."

"I think I'll stand, thanks."

"Fair enough." He kept his voice low so that I had to lean in to hear him. "Shifter Unlimited acts as a go-between, matching shifters with job placements that can be... financially lucrative."

"I'm not sure I understand." I found myself lowering into the chair without deciding to. I couldn't help it, it was like William's eyes were drawing me in.

"My company has been hired by the FBI."

"The FBI?!" I squeaked. I didn't like where this was heading. I could feel a cold sweat prickling at my hairline. My experience with government officials wasn't the best. They tended to be nothing more than a disappointment.

William nodded, his eyes intense. "Yes, they would like to offer a job to a man of your... talents."

"Talents? As a shifter?" I raised an eyebrow. "Who the hell needs a sloth shifter? That makes zero sense."

"I'm sorry, I'm not at liberty to discuss the job with you. All I ask is that you come with me to meet with them. Listen to what they have to say, and if it sounds like a good offer, the job is yours."

"I already have a job," I muttered. It didn't pay a ton, waiting tables at Fat Pizza, but it paid the bills. Plus, Pop was like family. I couldn't just leave without notice.

William seemed to see where my mind was going. "You wouldn't need to worry about your job. We would make sure it's still here when you get back, and we'd have someone step in to fill your shifts for you."

"Wow, you really have it all covered." I crossed my arms across my chest and leaned back in the chair.

He offered a casual shrug. "I'm good at what I do." It didn't come across as cocky; he was just stating a fact.

There was something about the alpha that I found soothing. I trusted him, even though I didn't know a thing about him. Sure, I could turn down his offer. He would get up and walk away, and I would likely never see him again. Or... I could spend an hour or two with this man, even if it was just breathing in that mouth-watering aroma.

"When do we go?" I asked.

"Whatever works for you."

"I'm off at eight."

He gave a tight nod, but when I stood up to go back to work, he stopped me. "Can I actually get a pizza? If I'm hanging out for your shift, I might as well eat."

True to his word, he stuck around for the entirety of my shift. And he wasn't even a cheapskate ordering free drinks and breadsticks. By eight, he'd polished off three pizzas, and he even ordered a fourth to take with him. When I ran his credit card, he tacked on a more-than-generous tip.

He didn't say anything when I showed up at his table after my shift. He simply threw on his jacket, grabbed his pizza box, and led the way to the door. Out front was a black sedan with heavily tinted windows.

Gods, this was how people disappeared, into unmarked vehicles, never to be seen again.

I wasn't exactly the most trusting person ever. I analyzed William as he held open the door for me. His posture was rigid, but nothing about him said criminal. And believe me, I knew criminals when I saw them. A bitter taste coated the back of my tongue.

He noticed my apprehension and said simply, "You can trust me."

His words rang true. I slid into the buttery-leather seat and held my breath. *Here goes nothing.*

TWO
WILLIAM

Brandon was obviously nervous, his eyes darting all over, biting his thumbnail down to the quick, but could I really blame him? I was surprised that he even got into the car with me, to be honest. I wasn't the kind of guy who automatically instilled trust in others.

I pulled the car into the underground parking, the light shifting from fading sunlight to flickering fluorescents.

"Where are we?" Brandon asked.

"FBI Headquarters." I'd told him this was where we were going, but I understood if he needed confirmation. He'd been distracted the whole drive over.

Honestly, I was just glad he broke the silence. "Thanks for doing this," I told him in an attempt to keep the conversation going.

"Hmm? Yeah. Sure." He nibbled on his lip, but not in a sexy way. More like an anxious way. If he kept it up, he was going to make himself bleed.

He nodded absently, taking in the nondescript cars parked in tidy rows. I pulled into a visitor spot and got out of the car and walked around to Brandon's side. For a moment, I wasn't sure if he would refuse to get out. I wasn't allowed to physically force him to come with me, though the thought of placing my hands on his body was definitely attractive. Force, no, but I could find other ways to persuade him.

The door popped open and he stepped out, bringing a waft of his scent out with him. I was no shifter, but even as limited as my human senses were, the aroma was nearly overpowering. I'd read something about how sloths had scent glands and secreted hormones. Maybe that was why my cock was responding to him. It certainly wasn't because of his tight ass in those pants... or the way his shirt hugged his shoulders...

I gulped and looked away. I gestured with my arm

towards the elevator, and Brandon turned to lead the way. It was purely selfish allowing him to go first like this; I just wanted to ogle him from behind. When I thought of sloths, I thought of lazy creatures, slightly bulbous, with disproportionately long limbs, but Brandon... was none of those things. If I didn't know any better, I would've pegged him as a cheetah, maybe. Definitely a predatory cat of some kind.

We rode up to the fourth floor in silence, but I found myself wishing we could be trapped in here for a little longer. I had to admit, I liked being in the enclosed space with him, and when the elevator gave a ding and opened to a room full of cubicles, a sense of dread settled over my shoulders.

Agent Nicholas Strait was the man I'd been assigned to help. I didn't like him. There was something about the alpha that rubbed me the wrong way. If I had hackles, they would be raised.

I led the way this time, down the hallway. I swore I could feel Brandon's eyes checking me out... but maybe it was just wishful thinking. I gave a sharp knock on the door, and a voice called, "Come in."

I opened the door to Agent Strait's office. The last of the day's sunlight filtered in through the windows, and I found myself squinting. Damn him with his corner office.

"Brandon Mills," Strait said, rising from his chair and coming out from behind his desk. "Thank you for coming in today."

"My pleasure," he said curtly, accepting Strait's extended hand for a shake, but I didn't get the sense that there was any pleasure at all involved in his being here. He'd been much more relaxed at the restaurant, and even in the car, but as soon as we stepped in the government building, he'd tensed up.

"Can I get you anything?" Strait offered. My eyes followed the way his touch lingered on Brandon's hand. "Coffee? Tea? Or are you hungry? I can get a sandwich delivered for you."

"No, thanks. I'm just here because William told me you had a job offer for me."

"Yes, of course. Straight to the point, I like that." He was still holding Brandon's hand.

My anger began to simmer. Why was Strait being so nice? He'd never offered me so much as a breath mint. I stepped forward and whipped my hand toward him, hoping to force him into letting go of Brandon's hand to shake mine instead. "Nice to see you again, Agent Strait. I'll take a coffee."

His eyes narrowed just slightly at me. "William." Damn him, we were most certainly not on a first-name basis. He was totally using it to undermine my authority here. Granted, I had no specific authority in this building at all, other than working as an intermediary between them.

Strait let go of my hand quickly and turned back to Brandon. "Please, why don't you come and have a seat."

Brandon moved forward and sat gingerly on the edge of the chair. "Can you just tell me what this is all about? I have stuff to do."

"Of course," Strait said softly, his voice like liquid charm. Damn him and his velvety voice.

I didn't want Strait paying such close attention to Brandon, and I didn't like how this made me feel. I gritted my teeth together, jealousy flaring hotly in my chest. I pulled a breath in through my nose and blew it slowly out between my lips. Brandon was not mine, I reminded myself. I had no right to be jealous.

And besides, it wasn't like Brandon was showing any interest in Strait anyway. His back was rigid and his muscles taut. He looked half ready to bolt instead.

I noticed there was only the one chair. How convenient. And Strait didn't bother getting my coffee, either. I moved closer and positioned myself close to Brandon's side. I couldn't sit beside him, but I hoped I could help put him at ease.

Brandon peeked at me from over his shoulder, and I saw him sag a little in relief. No matter that he wasn't mine, it seemed that I could at the very least bring him comfort. That was a small win, in my books, and I flashed Strait a satisfied grin.

Too bad he wasn't even looking at me. He only had eyes for Brandon.

THREE

BRANDON

"WE NEED YOUR HELP," AGENT STRAIT BEGAN. He leaned his elbows on the desk in front of him and steepled his hands, making him look like he was trying to portray a serious role, but it came across as overdone instead, and I nearly snorted a laugh. This guy was like a bad caricature of an FBI agent.

I knew I should be listening to what he had to say. This was a job offer, after all, and if the money was decent, I should at least have an idea about what was expected of me. The problem, however, was that William was standing just behind my left shoulder. I could sense his presence. No, more than that. I could feel the heat coming off his body. His crotch was nearly level with my shoulder. In fact... it would take very little effort to bend my head a little lower and—

"What do you think?" Strait interrupted my fantasy, and I snapped up in my seat.

"Uh, what do I think?"

I was worried about having to admit I wasn't listening, but Strait gave a little frown. I didn't have to admit it, he already knew. He plucked a pen from a cup on his desk and wrote something on a piece of paper. He slid it my way, and I picked it up, staring at the dismal offer of money.

"That's it?" I asked. I wasn't sure what I'd been expecting exactly, but when a government agency made a deal, I'd been hoping for a couple more zeroes.

"I'm afraid we're working on a limited budget," he admitted with a sheepish shrug, but I knew there was more money to be had. It all depended on how desperate he was. Too bad I hadn't been listening to the job description.

"And what would I have to do again?" I said.

"We need intel," he said slowly, as if speaking to a child. "We've been trying to get information on this guy for years, but he's a tough nut to crack. Every time we manage to get an agent undercover, they disappear."

"So, they're dead," I said sharply. Best not to sugar-coat it.

Strait winced. He didn't want me thinking about the risks, and about how they weren't worth that paltry sum he was offering. "That is the assumption."

"What the hell do you guys think I can do that your top agents couldn't? I'm just a waiter; I don't have any special training."

"Maybe not, but you do have a certain ability that could help us infiltrate his home." When I didn't immediately connect the dots, he elaborated. "We've had word that the man's daughter, Lily, has asked for a pet sloth for her birthday."

"And whatever Lily wants, Lily gets?" I intuited.

"Exactly." He gave a slow nod.

I wanted to know William's opinion on this matter. He'd been awfully quiet since we entered into this discussion. If it was his job at Shifters Unlimited to coordinate this kind of thing, then he must've been through the process a hundred times. Was this riskier than most jobs? Or was it no big deal? And should I ask for more money?

"Sooo..." I drawled. "You want me to play the role of pet for a little girl... and get intel for you guys?" I raised a brow, making sure I had this right.

"Yes, that's the gist of it." He was trying to play this off as casual, but there was one thing I'd noticed he was clearly avoiding.

"And who is this guy? You haven't mentioned his name."

Strait cleared his throat and refused to look me in the eye. Was it that bad? "Uh, you've probably never heard him, uh... it's..." His voice trailed off into mumbles.

"What was that? I couldn't quite catch it."

Strait pursed his lips and blurted, "Leo Vala."

"Big Daddy?" I barked out, my eyes going wide. "You want me to sneak into the home of Leo 'Big Daddy' Vala?" My mouth went dry and my stomach clenched tight. No. It couldn't be... the coincidence was too much.

"I assure you—"

"I'll do it," I interrupted. I didn't need to hear Strait's bullshit, downplaying Vala's reputation. That he wasn't really as dangerous as some claimed. He didn't actually have people executed for the smallest wrongdoing, like standing too close or breathing the same air.

I didn't need to hear it, because I knew exactly how bad Vala was. I had firsthand experience.

"I'm sorry, did you say you'll do it?" Strait's lips were slowly sliding into a tentative grin. He'd clearly been prepared for a long negotiation. This was my chance to demand more money.

But...

It was no longer about the money. Fine, I had come along with William because I thought that a little bit of extra money would be nice. It was all about a paycheck. But not anymore. The money didn't matter.

This was personal.

I would do this one for free.

"Wonderful!" Strait clapped his hands together and stood. "William will draw up the contract and give you all the details. Feel free to use the office. I'll step out and let you have some privacy."

He hurried out of the room, obviously worried that I might change my mind before I'd signed the paperwork.

I turned to William. His eyes were boring into mine as though he could see straight through to my soul.

I hope that's not true, I thought, *because he might not like what he finds.*

FOUR

WILLIAM

BRANDON'S BODY LANGUAGE DID A FULL ONE-eighty. At first, he'd barely been listening to Strait as he spoke. He seemed distracted and almost bored, but then suddenly, it was as though he'd sat on an electric cattle prod. His hands were white-knuckled on the chair's armrests, and his back was ramrod straight. There was practically an electric charge

"You should've asked for more money," I scolded him. Didn't he know the first rule about a contract like this? Never take the first offer. "It's not too late. I could go and—"

"No," he snapped. His eyes were blazing with a fierce anger, and I wished I could ask what that was all about. Had I done something wrong? I didn't think it was me, however, that had dragged this reaction out of him. Something Strait had said. Something about Leo Vala.

I swallowed down my curiosity. It wasn't my place to pry. In fact, it was against Shifters Unlimited policy. Privacy was given the strictest regulation. I gave a sharp bob of my head and moved around the desk to sit in Strait's chair.

This didn't feel right. I was too far from Brandon, and the desk was between us. It itched at my insides, so I stood up and rolled the chair around to the other side where I could sit by Brandon's side. I was close enough that our knees were nearly touching.

"Lily is seven," I began to outline the details, while I pulled the contract from my briefcase and laid it on the desk. "Her mother died when she was three, so it's just been her and her dad, and he'll do anything to keep his little girl happy. Her birthday is next week, and she told Leo that she wants a sloth. He contacted an exotic pet dealer three days ago, which is where you come in. You shift into your animal, and then we will arrange for the dealer to pass you along, straight into Vala's house."

He gave a nod, but it looked like his teeth were

clenched. "So, if she'd asked for a tiger, or a shark, you would be talking to a different kind of shifter right now?"

"Theoretically, I guess, but I would like to think Leo Vala wouldn't buy those kinds of predators for his daughter. I mean, there has to be a line drawn somewhere, right?" I tried for a shrug, but it came off too stiff.

"You're wrong. There are no limits for Leo Vala." Brandon was practically vibrating with rage. His limbs were quivering, and a muscle in his jaw was ticking a beat.

Before I could stop myself, I reached a hand out and rested it on Brandon's thigh. He instantly stilled beneath my touch, and his eyes shifted up to meet mine.

"You don't have to do this," I whispered softly. The last thing I needed was the FBI storming in here and asking me to leave because I was undermining their investigation. My loyalty, however, was pledged to Brandon Mills. I would advocate for his safety at every turn, regardless of what Strait said. I didn't care about evidence for their case. I only cared about this omega sitting in front of me.

"You don't understand," he hissed. "I do have to do this. I don't have a choice."

I knew there was more to this than what I was seeing on the surface. I squeezed his leg, and he looked down to where our bodies were in contact. I moved to pull my hand away, but he jumped forward and clutched my hand in his own. "I—I can't do this without you." He seemed as surprised by his admission as I was.

"I'll be with you every step of the way," I assured him.

"You're coming to Vala's house too?" He quirked an eyebrow. "What kind of animal will you turn into?"

He knew I was human; he could likely smell it on me. "I'll be a phone call away. I'll stay close, maybe book a hotel room nearby. All you need to do is call me and I'll be there within minutes."

This wasn't my job. I was only supposed to be here to negotiate the job, and then I would be sent back home, reassigned to recruit the next shifter, satisfy the next contract. And the next, and the one after that. It wasn't my job to get attached to my clients...

Even as I reminded myself of the facts, my body had another path in mind. Brandon's skin was smooth and warm on mine, and I had visions of drawing him closer, wrapping him in my arms, trailing my lips down his neck. My cock gave a twitch, and I had to shift in the chair. It wasn't all lust, though. My heart, too, gave a lurch at the thought of leaving Brandon to face Leo Vala on his own.

"You'll be here for me?" he asked breathlessly.

"I'm not going anywhere." In my mind, I was already calling in for vacation time. I wasn't leaving town anytime soon.

Without letting go of my hand, Brandon picked up the pen and signed on the dotted line. Anxiety clawed at me. I wanted to tear the pen from his hand, throw it across the room, tear the contract in two, and then take Brandon far away from here, where I could keep him safe.

But something told me that Brandon didn't care about being safe. He was on a mission all his own, that had nothing to do with the FBI. And I would do whatever it took to give him what he needed.

FIVE
BRANDON

My body no longer existed beyond the twisting bundle of nerves that was my stomach. I wasn't cut out for this. Yes, turning into a sloth was second nature, but that wasn't what was so ill-fitting about this situation.

I was a waiter, for gods' sake! I wasn't a spy or an agent. I had no training. I didn't even know how to handle a gun... though, honestly, if I had to shoot a gun, it would be more of a concern that I only had three fingers—er, toes—on each limb while in sloth form. Kinda made it hard to squeeze a trigger with claws.

"Hey, you've got this." William's voice was like a balm to the feverish flush burning across my skin. He hesitated, and then brought his hand up to trail a finger along my cheek. "You're sweating."

"Gee, thanks," I snorted, but I didn't pull away. I would take any form of contact from him right now, even if it was just to wipe away my sweat droplets.

"I didn't mean—" He shook his head. "I just wanted to help you relax."

"You do," I said with total seriousness. I reached out and squeezed his fingers. "You swear you'll be nearby?" The thought of doing this alone was slightly soothed by the thought of William being on the other end of the microphone.

Speaking of the microphone... Agent Strait sauntered into the room. He was all smiles today, since this was him essentially getting exactly what he wanted, and like a child, he had no problem gloating. If I weren't so damned determined to send Big Daddy to prison, I would turn this job down just to see Strait's face crumple. That guy was seriously irritating.

Strait held up his hand, and there, pinched between his fingers, was something that looked like a tooth.

Not human, but sloth. The microphone that would slip over my real tooth and allow me to transmit everything that was happening in the room with me.

"It's time," Strait said. He was practically skipping. Ugh.

With trembling fingers, I reached for the buttons of my shirt. William turned away to give me privacy, but Agent Strait didn't seem to regard this as a personal moment, but rather a professional one. He was set to watch the show. "Do you mind?" I spat.

"Oh." He gave a little frown and then turned his back.

I wouldn't have minded William watching...

I quickly undressed, folding my clothing into a neat stack, and then let the shift take over my body. This sterile back room didn't seem the proper place for a sloth, and I longed for a tree to climb, some leaf cover. I was a natural prey to nearly all animals, and most of my defense tactics involved camouflage. There was nowhere here for me to hide.

I reached out a claw and snagged William's pant leg. He turned and looked down at me. "Oh, Brandon," he whispered and then lowered himself down to my level. "May I pick you up?" he asked.

Wow, no one had ever asked that before. When people saw the poor, defenseless sloth, their first instinct was to handle it. I felt a wave of appreciation for this alpha. I dipped my chin in a nod, and he carefully wrapped his arms around me.

Nuzzling into his chest was like some kind of guilty pleasure, but I refused to feel even an ounce of guilt. He didn't seem to mind at all, so I would take everything I could get.

"Okay, microphone time." Strait interrupted my cuddle time and came at me with the fake tooth. I turned my chin away at the last moment. "You need to wear this. It's for your own safety," he huffed. I didn't want that man's hands anywhere near me. He moved in again, and I kept my mouth clamped shut.

"Maybe... I could?" William suggested.

Strait sneered at William but darted a look between us and grudgingly slapped the tooth down into William's hand.

I obediently opened and allowed him to press the fake tooth down over mine, like a cap. I was borderline tempted to lick his finger—I wanted to suck that finger and so much more—but that kind of thing might freak him out. He wasn't a shifter, and humans often had a hard time looking at our animal and seeing the human inside the creature.

William ran his hand along the fur of my neck. "There, how's that?" he murmured, and I leaned into his hand.

A tight pinch at the back of my neck had me flinching, and I couldn't stop the high-pitched squeal from being torn from my throat. That would be the tracking device being implanted under the skin.

"Hey!" William snapped at Agent Strait. "A little warning would've been nice."

"We don't have time for warnings." Strait scooped me out of William's arms and carried me over to the cage. He stuffed me in without being gentle.

I disliked this guy even more by the second.

The cage snapped shut with a clang and he passed me to a man in a rumpled suit. "Go," he instructed.

I kept my eyes locked on William for as long as I could. He opened his mouth to say something, but his words were lost when the door closed between us.

William, I called, but it came out as a soft squeak.

I was loaded into a vehicle and driven across town. Money exchanged hands, and soon enough, I found myself in the exotic pet dealer's warehouse. The cages were all too small to house these beautiful animals. There were brightly colored parrots and venomous snakes, geckos and spiders. I saw the large eyes of a slow loris, the oversized ears of a fennec fox, and even a penguin! Who kept a penguin as a pet?

I had been joking about the tiger, but I could see a large striped cat in a cage at the back. Who was this dealer, and why weren't the FBI doing something to bring him down? Why stop at Big Daddy Vala?

I made a vow. When this was all over, I would personally make it my mission to ensure this dealer would see the inside of a cell.

I didn't have to wait long. The door swung open and a large man came in. I recognized him immediately.

Leo "Big Daddy" Vala. My blood boiled. It was a good thing I was in sloth form, because I wouldn't have been able to hide the seething rage I felt otherwise. This piece of shit took everything from me. I bit down so hard I tasted blood.

Following behind Leo was his entourage, a couple of overweight, balding men in expensive suits.

"You got my sloth?" His voice was like gravel tumbling around in a cement mixer.

"Yes, sir. It's right here," the pet dealer said. He was practically groveling; I wouldn't have been surprised if he'd gotten down on his knees.

I wished I had more teeth to grind as Vala brought his face down to mine. "He's gentle?" he asked, looking over at the dealer. "I don't want to give my daughter a feral sloth."

"Yes, sir. As gentle as can be. I would trust him with a baby." As if this dealer had any clue about my temperament; I'd been here all of ten minutes. Good thing I could play the part.

"Fine. Pay the man," Vala said to one of his goons. They reached into their coat and pulled out a fat envelope, passing it over.

Just like that, a sloth was bought and sold. I wondered briefly how much my life was worth.

How much had Vala decided my father's life was worth?

SIX

WILLIAM

"Are you even listening to me?"

"Huh? Oh, yeah. Totally." I hadn't been, and we both knew it.

Damn this video call. Couldn't this meeting be done over the phone like normal people? Instead, over video, I could see how Jonathan narrowed his eyes at me.

"Uh huh. And what was I talking about?" he asked.

"Uhhh..." Shit. I wracked my brain, trying to piece together bits of the conversation into something that made sense. "The client needs... bananas... for the ape shifter?"

Jonathan burst out laughing. "Where they hell did you get that? We were talking about the lemur shifter at the zoo in Seattle."

"What? Really? I could've sworn I heard bananas."

"Where is your head at?" I was lucky Jonathan wasn't the type to get angered easily. He was taking over some of my upcoming clients so I could take a long-overdue holiday, and I really needed his help with this. *Holiday*... that was what I told my boss when I called in my request, at least. This holiday wasn't even a little bit relaxing. I could've been lounging on a beach somewhere, sipping mai tais. Instead, I was hunched over my laptop in a grungy motel room, gnawing on my fingernails.

"Uh, it's nothing," I said adamantly.

"It's not nothing." Jonathan tapped a finger on his chin. "Methinks it's a guy."

"What?" I squeaked, and the high pitch of my denial brought to mind the sound that Brandon had made when his cage was being carried away from me. My heart gave a pitter-pat in response. "There's no..." I couldn't bring myself to deny it. "Okay, fine. It's a guy."

"Ooh, yeah? Tell me all about him. Is it anyone I know? Wait! Don't tell me, is it a client?" He was practically bouncing in his seat at the promise of juicy gossip.

He was fishing for details, and a little alarm bell dinged in my head. I needed to keep Brandon safe at any cost, but what even were the rules about his identity right now? It wasn't like his human form was undercover, just his sloth, but just in case, I wasn't about to let any details of the job slip to Jonathan.

"He's just a guy I met at a restaurant." There, that was vague enough.

"That's it? That's all you're gonna give me to go on? You're no fun." He stuck out his lip in a fake pout.

"Well..." I had to throw him a bone—and if I were being honest with myself, I wanted to talk to someone about the way he made me feel. "He's actually why I'm taking a little holiday." Not a lie. "I —I really like him. There's just something about him. I'm not sure if this relationship will go anywhere, and I don't have a clue how he feels about me, but I think I owe it to myself to find out what it could be." I practically gasped when I finally got the words out. Did I just say relationship?

Where had that come from? And why did I feel like it was the truth?

Jonathan made an aww sound. "That is so sweet! I wish I had a guy to woo me."

Was that what I was doing? Didn't wooing involve flowers and fancy dinners? Maybe a box of chocolates. I was fairly certain there was nothing romantic about listening for an SOS call from a secret tooth microphone.

"There you go again," Jonathan said with a sigh.

"What?"

"I've been talking for five minutes, and you're just over there smiling and nodding." I offered a grim smile. I hadn't even noticed the conversation pick back up, but he held up a hand to stop any attempt at an apology. "Don't worry about it. I think it's cute. Don't stress about a thing on this end. These are easy jobs, but I'll send you an email if I run into any issues. Sound good?"

"Yeah, thanks for doing this, Jonathan."

"No problem. You can return the favor when I find my sexy alpha and need to disappear for a week." He gave me a wink. Damn video calls.

"Deal."

We disconnected the call, and as soon as the laptop was closed, I scrambled to bring the FBI-issued earpiece back up to my ear. I didn't like it when I couldn't hear Brandon's soft breath. There hadn't been much to hear so far, it had only been a few hours, but that didn't mean that it couldn't go sideways at any moment.

Just as I hooked it into my ear, there was a high-pitched squeal through the speaker, and I was up off the bed in a flash. Brandon was in danger!

I was halfway to the door when the squeal tapered off, and I heard a tinkling voice say, "Is that for my birthday? What is it? Can I open it now?"

A grumbling voice said, "No peeking, Lily. It's a surprise, you know that."

I sagged down to the floor, right there, and pressed my forehead into the Berber carpet. Gods, my heart was in my throat.

I listened for another moment as the man who must be Leo Vala wandered off, trying to convince his daughter that she had to wait patiently for her party. Silence descended again, and I swallowed back the bile as the adrenaline drained out of my body and left me feeling nauseated.

I tried to imagine what Brandon was feeling right now. Was he nervous? Was he afraid? Or maybe angry...? I thought of the way his teeth gnashed and his eyes flared at the mention of Leo Vala.

As if Brandon knew I was thinking about him, there was a gentle purring sound.

"Hang on, Brandon. I'm here," I whispered, willing the words to somehow travel out of my motel, down the street, and into the Vala compound. "I've got you."

The reality of the situation began to sink in as the feeling returned to my limbs. The adrenaline had sent me straight to the very edge of my sanity, and the relief had literally knocked me on my ass. Brandon wasn't just some ordinary client. Somehow, he had become so much more.

SEVEN

BRANDON

I WASN'T SURE WHICH WAS WORSE... THE anticipation, or coming face to face with the true horror of my situation. Oh gods. There were no words to describe it.

"Dadddddyyyyyy!"

When the cloth was finally whipped away from the cage, I found myself staring straight into the wide eyes of seven-year-old Lily. Her tiny, balled fists were waving frantically, and I was fairly certain the neighborhood dogs were burying their heads under pillows. Me, however, couldn't do anything to protect my ears from that glass-shattering pitch.

Big Daddy Vala was beaming. There was no doubt that he loved his little girl, that he was willing to do anything to make her smile. Too bad he didn't give a shit about anyone else.

I didn't know anything about Lily beyond her age, but how corrupt could a child be? She was most likely innocent in all this, as innocent as I'd been at her age. All she knew was that she loved her daddy, and that he just gave her exactly what she's asked for. A sloth.

She began to fumble with the cage door, trying frantically to get through the bars to me. Leo came over to help. "Easy, honey, you don't want to pinch your fingers in the bars."

"Does he have a name, Daddy?" She pulled her hands back and let him work the clasp, but she wasn't being patient about it.

"Hmm, what do you think about the name... Leo?"

"No, Daddy, that's your name!"

"Okay, what about... Bobby?" He was just trying to distract her at this point, while he opened the cage.

"Nooooo, that's Uncle Bobby's name!" Lily was giggling and looked over her shoulder at the man behind Leo, who I assumed was Uncle Bobby, and he gave her a wink.

Finally, the cage was open, and Lily practically crawled straight in with me in her rush. "Easy, honey." Leo tugged her back and reached into the cage. "I'll get him for you."

My stomach clenched tight at the feel of his hands on me. I wanted to claw at his eyes, dig my claws into his flesh. Unfortunately, sloths aren't built for that kind of defense. My muscles were designed for hanging from tree branches for hours at a time, or maybe slowly crawling across the ground, but certainly not for brute strength. The second I made an attempt, Leo would just wring my neck, and that would be the end of that.

No, I would have to play the long game. So, in this case, I forced myself to go limp and be drawn out of the cage. Lily's touch felt entirely different to her father's, but not in a good way. Her arms wrapped tight around me and she squeezed.

Gods, were my eyes bugging out? I let out a weak squeak, and I could see the men exchange a glance behind Lily's shoulder. Nobody made a move to save me, though. Lily was thoroughly spoiled in the worst way. Everyone was terrified to tell her no, but whether that was to avoid the wrath of Leo himself, or if the seven-year-old was even worse, I couldn't be sure.

"Honey, do you remember what I told you? You have to be gentle." I kind of hated that it was Big Daddy who came to my rescue.

Lily obediently loosened her grip, and I filled my lungs with precious oxygen. My head flopped down on her shoulder in my relief, and she seemed to think that meant it was hug time. She rocked me back and forth like a baby doll. "I love him, Daddy! I'm gonna call him Lawrence. Booboo, for short."

"Okay, honey. I'm glad you like him."

"Not just like. Loooooove." She forgot to be gentle for a moment, and her arms gave a rib-cracking clamp around my torso. One more squeak and she quickly rectified her hold. At least she could be trained. And hopefully, after the novelty wore off, she would get tired of carrying me around.

"Look, Uncle Bobby!" She swung me around to stare up at the rotund man with the slicked-back hair. "Did you see my sloth?"

"Yeah, hon, he's awesome."

"He certainly is," she said with a sharp nod. She then took me around the entire party and introduced me to each of her friends. Most of these "friends" just seemed to be other associates of her father's, so I made sure to hold my mouth open so the FBI could hear each and every one of their voices. I couldn't forget that the whole point to me being here was to take down Leo Vala, but it wouldn't hurt if we could snag a few more of these guys for something.

This wasn't your average birthday party. It was over-the-top gaudy, to the extreme. There were pink taffeta bows and balloons galore, as well as a massive spread of food and a crystal punch bowl filled with some kind of pink fizzy punch. Outside the patio doors I could see a petting zoo and saddled ponies.

I got a pretty good view of the house layout as we paraded around. I kept my eyes open for a room that could be Vala's office; maybe I could sneak out after everyone was asleep and look for evidence of his crimes.

I needed to hurry this along. How long was I supposed to stay here, exactly? A week? A month? Hell, if they didn't find evidence to put Vala away, I could be stuck here for years! That wasn't an option.

This was bullshit. I could feel my lips pull back in disgust, but luckily, the expression looks much the same as every other emotion on a sloth.

"Look, Daddy! He's smiling!"

"Of course he is. He's happy to be with you," Leo said, beaming his gold-capped smile.

What the hell have I gotten myself into? I had to admit that I didn't give this plan enough proper thought. Maybe I could've just let it all go. Let go of the past, let Leo go unpunished for everything he'd done. Maybe I could be lying in bed with William at this very moment, feeling nothing but bliss.

No. That wasn't ever going to happen. Even if I didn't believe that Big Daddy Vala deserved to burn in Hell, it was certainly too late to change my mind now. I hoped William was out there like he'd promised he would be. I could withstand this if he was there.

EIGHT

WILLIAM

It was official. This was killing me. Brandon wasn't here, and I was dying.

All I did for hours at a time was pace the very short length of this room. Every single sound through the earpiece had my heart galloping in my chest. I couldn't eat, I couldn't sleep. And even though he was just down the street, he might as well have been in Timbuktu, for how many barriers were standing between us.

I listened to the birthday party for ages. It was mostly just people chatting, and I was pretty sure I heard a horse whinny in the background, some water splashing, maybe a pool. I relaxed a bit because I knew as long as I was listening to Lily's voice, it meant that Brandon was safe. I never would have imagined that a rambunctious child would be the most trustworthy person in a room, as wild and unpredictable as they could be, but I found myself relaxing into the sound of her voice.

But then I heard Leo Vala saying it was time for bed. My eyes darted over to take a peek at the window, and sure enough, it was slowly getting dark outside. As the silence descended, and the darkness of night began to cloak the street outside, my mood took a dive. It sank straight down into my toes. I needed reassurance that Brandon was okay.

It was near 2am by the time I slipped out the door and crept down the street towards the Vala compound. I did my best to look like I was out for a casual stroll, but at this time of night, anyone walking the streets looked suspicious.

The house was dark, but I kept to the shadows as much as I could. I knew from the layout of the house that Lily's room was around the back, and I walked the perimeter of the fence until I was adjacent to her window. I told myself that I just needed to be close to him, to see with my own eyes that he was okay. I stepped behind a pillar and waited. I wanted to call out to Brandon, but that would be too dangerous for him.

Wait... was that movement? I squinted to peek through the gloom. Yes! There was definitely someone moving around in Lily's bedroom. I panted, my breath hot and dry, unsure of who would be in the room at this time of night. Should I call for backup?

Then a leg swung out the window. "What the—" It was a bare leg!

Another leg followed, and then a naked ass hanging over the sill. I watched in slack-jawed amazement as Brandon shimmied out the window and sprinted across the lawn toward me. He had a blanket wrapped around his shoulder, but it flapped in the breeze, giving me a full view of everything he had to offer.

"Damn," I whispered.

Brandon didn't even pause at the fence. He simply climbed up the vines and hurdled over to my side, landing beside me with a soft thump. "What are you doing?" I hissed. "Are you in danger?" I scanned the yard behind him for gun-toting mobsters, but he shook his head.

"I'm okay," he said. "I just saw you out here, and—I couldn't help myself. I needed to see you."

I quickly took off my jacket to wrap around his shoulders. "You must be cold."

A look crossed his face, and it made me blush for some reason. "You know, my legs are a bit chilly. Maybe you could offer me your pants."

Oh. He gripped the front of my shirt in his fingers and stepped closer. Since we were already tossing all rational thought out the window, I might as well throw caution to the wind as well. I reached my hands up to tangle them in his hair and drew his mouth closer to mine.

I gave a pause, waiting for him to tell me to stop, to step away, to shake his head... but everything about him said *yes, yes, yes*. I dipped my head down and pressed my mouth against his. I felt his lips parting to allow me entrance, and I slid my tongue in, a most intimate intrusion. The kiss deepened, and Brandon made a mewl in the back of his throat. He hooked a leg around my waist, pressing his growing erection into me. I was all too aware of the fact that he wasn't wearing any pants right now.

I knew with absolute certainty that if we didn't get somewhere private fast, I would take him right here on the boulevard.

I pulled back and grabbed his hand. "Come with me? Just for an hour," I whispered, and he nodded his head. I looked down to see that his other head was nodding too. I reluctantly wrapped the small blanket around his waist. The last thing we needed was to be picked up by a beat cop for public indecency.

And then we ran, faster than I have ever run before. I swear we broke the sound barrier in our rush to get back to my motel room.

This was dangerous. We were potentially ruining the entire undercover operation, but right now, the only covers I wanted him under were on my bed. Ironically enough, we didn't even make it to the bed. I slammed the door behind us, and then pressed Brandon up against the wall.

"Too many clothes," he mumbled against my lips. Since I assumed he meant me, I tore at my shirt and pants. My fingers felt clumsy and numb, but

Brandon was eager to help. Buttons went flying in all directions. Soon enough, I pressed against him, skin to skin, but even that wasn't close enough.

"I need to be inside you," I groaned.

Brandon nodded vigorously and ground his hips against mine. "Yes, that. Do it." I clutched at his ass and lifted him enough that he could wrap his legs around me. My hands were parting his ass cheeks, and all it took was a quick shift of my hips to bring my cock to line straight up with his puckered entrance.

"Gods, you're so slick," I moaned. I could feel the muscled ring of muscle flaring against the head of my dick, beckoning me in. Who was I to turn down such an invitation?

My fingers dug into Brandon's cheeks, and I thrust forward, slowly, as his channel relaxed to accommodate my girth.

Brandon threw his head back against the door with a thud. "Shiiiit." Just as I was fully sheathed in his slick ass, Brandon used his legs to raise himself up on my shaft.

Now I was the one throwing my head back. "That's so good, Brandon."

As he lowered himself back down, I met him half-way. This was so dangerous, but that only seemed to ratchet up the pleasure. Neither of us was going to last long. I moved inside him, faster, harder, until I was pistoning at a furious pace.

"Yes, William! Yes!" Brandon's ass clenched around my length and then his cock gave a spasm, and a white stream of cum spurted up between us, painting my chest with his ejaculation. It was enough to tip me over the edge. My balls clenched tight, and with a final pump, I unleashed myself into him, my knot expanding and filling every inch of him.

I lowered us down to the floor gently, and we lay there in a heap, entirely sated. I regretted nothing.

NINE

BRANDON

I cracked my eyes open and got hit with a momentary sense of panic. What time was it?! I hadn't meant to fall asleep. What if Lily noticed I was gone? She would tell her father, and there was no way I would be able to sneak back into the compound with them all on high alert, looking for a runaway sloth!

I bolted upright, my heart thrumming. The curtains were still dark. Phew! Still before dawn, I was safe... probably.

"Hey, it's okay. It's still early."

I looked down into William's eyes, shining in the dark. "You're awake," I said, stating the obvious.

"Yeah, I didn't want to disturb you, but I made sure to stay awake so that you didn't oversleep."

"Thanks." I peeked at the digital clock. 3:47am. "We still have some time," I said with a wink, which he likely couldn't see in the shadowed room. His arm snaking up my thigh told me he caught the drift, though.

"And what do you suggest we do with our time?" His voice sent vibrations through me, and I lowered myself down, pressing my chest against his.

"We could play cards," I offered, pressing my lips against his throat.

"Hmm, good idea." He laced his fingers through my hair and gave a delicious tug. "Though I'm more of a board game man, myself."

"I do love a good round of Twister." I gasped when he worked his way down and lathed my nipple with his tongue, sending a shiver all the way down to my toes.

"This kind of twister?" he murmured and then gave my nipple a tweak.

I yelped. "Hey, gentle with those, mister. I might need them one day."

He chuckled, but the laugh soon turned to a groan as his hand slid around to the back of my thigh to find a trail of slick. "Oh, omega mine, how I wish we had more time."

"We can be fast," I panted.

William stilled for a second—just one—before rolling on top of me. His arms held me beneath him, and I decided this was very much the kind of cage that I preferred. "When this is over," he pledged, "when there aren't any deadlines or anyone else's expectations getting in the way... I am going to take my time with you."

"I'm already looking forward to it. But until then, fuck me already!" I gyrated my hips, grinding my cock against his abs and teasing his dick with my dripping hole.

"My pleasure," he said. He moved above me, filling me in a way that no alpha had ever done before.

Turned out it was very much my pleasure as well.

"WHEN WILL I SEE YOU AGAIN?" William asked.

We were standing back outside the compound. It was still dark, but only just. I could sense the sun approaching the horizon, and I knew that I couldn't wait any longer. It was time to go back.

"I'm not sure. I have no clue what Agent Strait's plan is. He wants me to report back to him when I find something, so I guess it will depend on what I find. Maybe I should start looking for evidence." I gave a shrug, trying to look casual, but in fact, the mere thought of digging around Vala's house had me wanting to barf on my bare feet.

"Be careful," William said with feeling. "I couldn't stand if anything happened to you." I could see the words that were threatening to spill from his lips, oaths of undying devotion. It was too early for big feelings like this, but you couldn't tell your heart what to feel. William placed his hands on either side of my face and kissed me, slowly, passionately.

"Careful, or we'll have to go back to the motel to take care of this," I teased, wiggling my hips to set my erection swinging. The blanket I'd stolen was draped over my shoulders, and William's jacket was back on him where it belonged. I wished I could take it with me, to cuddle up in, wrapped in his scent while in my cage, but unfortunately, that wasn't possible. I had to go back to the compound exactly as I'd left... naked.

A quick peek through the bars of the fence showed me that the coast was clear. "I guess this is goodbye," I whispered, trailing my fingers over his stubbled jaw.

"No, it's a see-you-soon." One last kiss was all I could allow; otherwise, I might never find the courage to leave his side.

I hefted myself up and over the fence and dropped down to the lawn on the other side. While the dread began to settle back in place, there was a spark of something new inside me. It was just a twinkle of hope, but I clamped onto it with both fists. I could do this. I would find a way to put Vala behind bars, where he could no longer hurt anyone, and then I could return to William. We could start a relationship... maybe even have a future together.

The climb back in through the window was harder

than it had been to get out. I skinned my knees on the ledge and tumbled in with a thud. I heard a rustle of fabric and the patter of feet. I just barely managed to shift into my sloth before Lily came darting into the room.

"There you are!" she gasped. "How did you get out of your cage?" She picked me up into her arms and gave me another one of her signature squeezes. My eyes were about to pop out, but she luckily loosened her hold so she could gaze down into my face.

"I was so worried," she cooed. "I woke up and saw that you were gone, and I looked everywhere! I was just about to tell Daddy, but then he would be mad at me for not closing the cage properly."

Relief skittered through me. That would've been the end of me, if she'd woken up her father. It would've been impossible for me to sneak back in. I needed to be more careful in future... when I snuck out to see William again.

Because of course I would. I knew with certainty that I couldn't stay away. There would always be a next time.

TEN

WILLIAM

"Quit fidgeting," Agent Strait muttered. "You don't need to be here, you know."

"Yes, I know, and I appreciate you bringing me along." I tried to make my tone as flattering as possible. The last thing I needed was for Strait to cut me out of the loop. Technically, my role on this job was long over, but I suspected that Brandon had requested me specifically, as a dealbreaker.

Part of me wanted to boast about the connection Brandon and I shared. I wanted to rub Strait's nose in the fact that Brandon chose me... but then I reminded myself that I didn't want to bring attention to the fact that my omega had snuck out to see me. It was a risk to their investigation, and it probably wouldn't go over too well. It was a sure-fire way to get myself cut out, and I knew without a shadow of a doubt that Brandon needed me.

I did my best to settle myself, but I was restless. I knew that Brandon was just down the street, so close I could nearly taste him. My mouth watered at the thought of taking him into my mouth, coaxing his orgasm out of him until he emptied his load down my throat.

A sharp pain cut into my daydream. I was getting leg cramps.

We were wedged into a flower delivery van a block down from the Vala compound. We were keeping our distance, until we saw the front gates open and a black sedan cruise out.

"There they go," Strait said to the driver, who was dressed in the blue uniform of the florist. We'd waited until Vala and Lily were going out for a late dinner, to reduce the risk of them witnessing our meeting. Strait said their intel showed the house was now empty. "Pull up."

The driver turned the key and moved the van up until we were adjacent to the window where I'd seen

Brandon climb out last week. It was approaching full dark, but it was still a risk to him being seen sneaking out. The FBI had arranged for phones to ring in the homes all down the block, a survey asking about their internet provider, so that everyone was distracted and facing away from windows, right as Brandon hopped out.

I was out of the van's sliding door before I'd been given the all-clear, and I heard Strait hiss behind me. "Knowles!"

I met Brandon at the fence. He was dressed today, and I raised an eyebrow at his ill-fitting wardrobe choice.

He shrugged. "Trust me, I would prefer to be naked, but I thought it would be less suspicious for a neighbor to see some random man on the lawn, instead of a nudist. I grabbed this out of Vala's closet."

"I prefer you naked too," I said, and his cheeks glowed as he bit the inside of his cheek.

Strait came up beside me. He radiated rage, and I was sure to hear about it later, but for now, he was all business. "What have you got for me?" he asked Brandon.

Brandon pulled a few folded pieces of paper from his pocket and passed them through the bars. "There are some manifests for shipments coming in. There are drugs coming in on that first one, and guns on the second."

Strait unfolded them and scanned them quickly. "It's not enough. What else?" He looked back at Brandon, and my omega's shoulders sagged.

He sounded so dejected as he admitted, "That's it."

"That's it? No, you need to find more." Strait shoved the papers into his pocket and then crossed his arms across his chest.

I gritted my teeth to stop myself from slamming my fist into Strait's face. "He's doing the best he can," I snapped.

"Well, his best isn't good enough." Strait got up in my face, and Brandon's hand snaked through the bars to rest on my arm.

"Hey," he whispered. "It's okay. This was the deal. I knew what I was getting into." There was a dull luster to his eyes that told me he meant what he said.

"I'll find it. I'll do what I can to put Vala away for life."

I was so proud of Brandon. He was the bravest man I knew, and I wished I could wrap my arms around him and offer him comfort. But this was not the time or place. I had no idea when we would have the chance again, but I would wait as long as it took.

I gave his hand a squeeze. Strait observed the gesture without a word, but his lips thinned. He knew there was more between us than client and handler.

"Be careful," I whispered, hoping he understood all the words I couldn't say. "Call if you need me."

Brandon gave a nod and turned away, jogging back across the lawn and through the window.

We waited by the fence until Brandon was out of sight. The house remained dark and silent. So far, so good. We walked back to the van, and Strait put a hand on my chest to stop me. "You're too close to this case," he said.

There was no point in denying it, so I nodded slowly. "You're probably right, but you need me."

He opened his mouth to dispute, but I already knew what he was going to say. I cut him off, speaking over him. "Look, wouldn't you agree that you want Brandon to be motivated to get out of there? Focused on the job at hand?"

Strait nodded. "Are you saying you're his motivation?"

"I certainly don't hurt. Besides, I have a feeling I'm listening to that mic with a lot more diligence than any of your agents."

"Okay. Fair enough. Just don't distract him, or I'll have you out of here so fast, you'll have whiplash. Don't think I didn't notice your little sexy-time rendezvous." He tapped the back of his neck, right where they'd put the tracking device beneath Brandon's skin.

I pursed my lips. Strait said not to distract Brandon, but I liked to believe that I was helping him stay on task. "I'm glad we had this talk."

He rolled his eyes at me, and when I went to follow him into the van, he stopped me. "I think you can walk."

"But—" The door slid closed in my face.

Okay, so we weren't exactly on good terms, but we had an agreement. I couldn't ask for more than that.

I watched the van drive away and then began the walk back to my motel. I cast one final look over my shoulder at the Vala compound.

"Hang in there, Brandon," I whispered to myself. "I'm still here."

And I would be, for however long it took.

ELEVEN

BRANDON

"Uncle Bobby, will you come play with me?" The hope on Lily's face damn near broke my heart. She spent most of her days alone—except for me, of course, but I wasn't exactly the best company in my current form.

"Uh, sorry, sweetie. I'm a bit busy at the moment." There was a little quiver in his voice, and I took a moment to really look at the man.

He was dressed in a dark suit, which was pretty standard, but he wasn't as put together as usual. There was a light sheen of sweat on his brow, and his eyes were looking mighty shifty. He pulled a handkerchief from his pocket and dabbed at his forehead. "Maybe later, okay?" he said.

"Yeah. Whatever." Lily's shoulder slumped.

"Bobby," Leo barked from down the hall, "We gotta go." Bobby damn near jumped out of his skin.

"Yeah, boss. Coming."

As he scurried off, Lily plodded over to my cage. "I guess it's just you and me, Booboo." Even though she had officially dubbed me Lawrence, she only ever called me by my nickname. I didn't mind it so much.

Lily wasn't your average child. At times she seemed too childish, but I chalked that up to the fact that she never had the chance to play with children her own age. She was constantly surrounded by her father's guards and associates, and they all seemed to treat her like a baby. Most kids her age were more interested in cell phones and video games, but she just wanted a best friend, someone to talk to and adore. I guess that was my role now.

As she unhooked the clasp on my cage, I held my arms out for her. This brought a little smile to her face. "You're the bestest, most sweetest pet I've ever had," she whispered, nuzzling into me. "Too bad you stink."

Hey, I thought. *You try secreting oil from your back and see how good you smell.*

Although she complained about my stink, she didn't seem to care all that much. She still held me close, rocking me like a baby. The motion set my stomach churning, so I was glad when she finally set me down in the small wooden chair.

"Would you like some tea, Booboo?" She waited a beat as if listening to my answer. "Of course, that sounds wonderful. What a great idea!"

I had no clue what I'd suggested that was so wonderful, but she nodded sagely, so I was sure it was a very wise answer. She picked up her small teapot from the center of the table and poured me a cup of... well, it was nothing. Pretend tea, I guess, but I could imagine with the best of them.

Lily then placed a plastic scone on a dainty plate and slid it over beside the tea. "Hmm, something's missing." She tapped her chin, but by the mischievous glint in her eye, I knew she was just playing. She hopped up from her chair and grabbed a small box from on her bed. "Look what Daddy got you!" Whatever it was, Big Daddy Vala couldn't care less what about my wants or needs, but if it kept his little girl smiling, then it was hers. Or, in this case, mine.

She opened the box and pulled out a bright pink flower. "It's a hibiscus flower! Your favorite!"

It was not my favorite. Not even a little. I actually hated them, but I could hardly tell her I wanted lasagne instead. Ooh, or a nice juicy burger. Chips sounded good, or... my stomach gave a lurch as she put the flower on the plate in front of me and the scent wafted over me. My stomach twisted. Ugh. Maybe a ginger ale would be more fitting.

Lily propped her elbows on the table and watched me. "Why aren't you eating?" She picked up the flower and placed it to my lips.

Here goes nothing. I huffed out a small sigh and opened my mouth. She shoved that flower straight in, and I nearly gagged. I took the flower from her, so I could at least control how far down my gullet the petals went, but even then, the taste and aroma were overpowering.

For real sloths, hibiscus flowers were like the sweetest candy, but I just couldn't. When Lily turned away to pour her own tea, I discreetly dropped the flower to the floor.

Lily chattered away about her day, which sounded extremely boring. She was homeschooled by a tutor for a large part of the week, and that was pretty much it. Her entire social life revolved around imaginary tea parties with her pet sloth. Yesterday, she brought me down to their home movie theater to watch some animated movie; she thought I would like it because it had a sloth in it.

This wasn't the life for a child. She was incredibly sweet and intelligent and funny... so, why couldn't she be allowed to blossom and grow? She was kept confined within these walls, for her own protection, and she was suffocating. Her father wanted to keep her safe—and I understood that, I did—but there had to be more to life than this.

I gave a lot of thought about what would happen to Lily when they arrested her father. She would miss him, but it would be for the best. It had to be.

A woman popped her head in the door. I recognized her as someone who usually worked in the kitchen; she sometimes brought food for Lily. "Bedtime, Lily."

"Anna? Why are you here? Where's Daddy? Isn't he going to come tuck me in?"

"I'm sorry, dear, he got called out. It's just you and me tonight." A phone rang, and she pulled a cell phone out of her pocket. She turned her head to whisper into the phone, and I caught her saying, "I'll call you back in a minute, okay?"

Lily shoved back from the table, her small chair knocking back on the floor with a clatter. She didn't bother righting it, and instead stomped over and picked me up from my spot. She was clearly annoyed at being left alone yet again, but did she need to swing me around so quickly?

The lurching motion in her arms, paired with the hibiscus scent, had my stomach clenching tight. I couldn't stop my stomach from emptying right then and there, all over Lily's shirt.

"Ewww!" she shrieked. "Booboo barfed on me!"

Anna made a face and turned her head away. She gave a long-suffering sigh and checked her watch. She clearly had somewhere else she'd rather be. "Okay, let's get you cleaned up."

Lily put me back in my cage, more gently this time, probably because she didn't want me to throw up again. Then she left with Anna to get changed and wash up.

My stomach remained sour for the rest of the evening. Lily came back and crawled into bed, and the house went dark and silent. The moon slid across the sky outside.

My thoughts slithered through my mind in much the same way, slow and steady, from point A to point B... and the conclusion I came to just made me feel even more unsteady.

Sure, I was queasy, and there was a good chance that it was just from the hibiscus flower, but there were other reasons to feel sick. I'd been here for weeks... and I hadn't had a heat this whole time. And William and I hadn't been careful when we had sex. There was no way... was there?

Gods... was I pregnant?

TWELVE

WILLIAM

I THOUGHT I WAS DREAMING WHEN I HEARD MY name whispered over the microphone. I'd been here for weeks and had barely slept that whole time. I kept extending my holiday time, and lucky for me, Agent Strait was backing me up about it. I'd been listening to the earpiece for hours on end, so it was entirely possible that I'd drifted off, and Brandon pretty much came to life in my dreams as it was... but no, there it was again.

It wasn't a call for help—I was sure if he was any danger, he would be yelling or something. No, this was just the barest of whispers. It could almost be mistaken for static.

Just in case Brandon needed to see me, I headed straight out and walked briskly down the block to the compound. Sure enough, as soon as I approached the fence, Brandon was out the window and making his way across the lawn.

"You're not naked," I teased, though to be honest, I wouldn't have minded seeing more of him.

"No, we actually have to go to the store, so I figured clothes were a must."

"We're going shopping?" I looked around at the darkened street. "Not a lot open at this time of night."

"But a pharmacy would be." He raised a single eyebrow and said nothing more.

"Why would you need... Oh." Shit. Was he implying a pregnancy test? My jaw dropped, and Brandon bit down on his lip.

"Are you mad?"

"No, not even a little," I said honestly. "I mean, it's sooner than I would've planned, but..."

"But?" he asked, and his eyes shone with hope.

"But I would like to think we would've gotten there eventually, all on our own." I traced the line of his jaw with my finger. Either he'd been shaving or his human hair didn't grow while he was in sloth form.

"You mean it?" Brandon looked up at me, and I used that opportunity to lean in and press my lips to his.

"I do. Now, do you need me to get the test and bring it back for you? Will you be missed?"

"No, they're out for the night, and Lily's down for the count."

"Okay, then let's go get you a test so we can make plans for the future, one way or another." I took his hand in mine and we dashed down the street together.

There was a giddy sort of laughter bubbling up inside of me. Could Brandon really be pregnant? Me, a father. I told myself to slow down, we didn't know anything for sure yet, but by the time we bought the test and made our way to the motel, I was already thinking up names for this hypothetical baby.

"Hurry up and pee already!" I burst out as soon as we stepped into the room, and Brandon laughed nervously.

"I'm going, I'm going," he said with a wave of his hand and disappeared into the bathroom.

Those minutes felt more like hours—no, months! I know they say a watched pot never boils, but how does that apply to pregnancy tests? We sat next to each other on the bed, the test face down between us.

"Is it time yet?" I asked for the billionth time.

He blew out a breath. "No! I set the timer on your phone. It won't be ready until—"

He was interrupted by the timer giving its ding, and I leapt across the mattress and pounced on the plastic stick. I flipped it over and—had no clue what I was doing. "What am I looking for?" I asked.

Brandon picked up the box and looked at the back. "Uh, two lines?" he said, but he didn't seem certain.

"What does two lines mean? Pregnant or not pregnant?"

"Pregnant," he whispered. His hands were clasped tight together in front of him. What kind of test result was he hoping for?

I flipped the test his way and watched his reaction as he took in the lines. Lines, as in plural. "Pregnant," he gasped.

"Is this... good?" I wanted to scream the news from the rooftops, but I also needed to be here and support Brandon, no matter what he needed. If he was scared, then I would need to keep my excitement level down a notch. For now, at least.

"Yes," he said bluntly, but he was avoiding my eye. "But also no."

"Okay, let's talk it out. What's the bad part? We'll see if we can conquer that together."

Brandon latched onto my hand and interlaced our fingers. "Well, it's mostly just that I'm still under-cover at Vala's."

"Well, that's an easy one. They'll have to extract you. It's too bad for them, they'll just have to try to convict him on what you've given them so far."

Brandon was shaking his head furiously. "You don't get it," he moaned, tugging at his hair and rocking back and forth. "You don't know the whole story. My dad—" He gasped, and I crawled over and wrapped my arms around him.

"Tell me."

"Leo Vala, he... he killed my dad when I was eight. We'd hit some hard times, and my dad borrowed some money. Just enough to get the bills under control, it wasn't that big a deal, but then he lost his job and couldn't pay him back. And Leo killed him. Like he was nothing."

I shushed him gently and rubbed his back, and when he angled his face up to mine, I wiped the tears from his cheeks.

"Don't you see? I need to put Vala away, and this might be my only chance."

My heart was aching for Brandon. "I'm sorry, I didn't know."

He shook his head gently. "This baby... they're everything to me. I need to be there for them and to keep them safe. To me, that means putting Vala behind bars where he belongs. The world will be a better place without him in it."

I was so torn. "Okay," I said reluctantly. I trusted him to be careful, but the thought of our child being at risk had me clenching my teeth.

"And maybe... how would you feel about Lily coming to live with us?" he asked.

"Lily? I don't think that's not how it works."

"She doesn't have anyone, William. She's alone in that house, surrounded by criminals and servants. She needs us."

While I couldn't dispute that fact, I wasn't at all sure that the rules worked that way. Right now, though, Brandon needed all the support that I could give him, so I said, "The more the merrier."

This brought a beaming smile to his face. "Really? Do you mean that?"

"Absolutely."

Brandon tackled me, pushing me back on the bed. His fingers began working my buttons.

"What are you doing?" I asked, though it was obvious. Even if he weren't undressing me, the massive boner pushing at his pants was quite a clue to how he was feeling.

"I'm celebrating. Can't you tell?"

"Congratulations," I told him, and then used my body to say the rest.

W ILLIAM'S HANDS WERE EVERYWHERE AT ONCE; tugging at my clothes, trailing down my torso, squeezing at my thighs. And when our clothes were finally thrown into a pile on the floor, his hands went straight to where I needed them to be.

I gasped at the sensations. His right hand wrapped around my shaft, pumped it once, twice. His left hand was busy too, sliding around to my seeping entrance.

"Tell me what you want," he said, his deep voice invoking dirty thoughts in my mind.

"I want you," I panted.

"Be more specific," he said with a chuckle.

"How about I show you instead." I took his hands in mine, then leaned forward, pinning them above his head. The look in his eyes was pure sin. We gazed into each other's faces as I raised my hips, tilting them just right.

A soft breath escaped his lips when I positioned the head of his cock right at my hole, dripping slick down his length. To his credit, he didn't move an inch. It wouldn't have taken much for him to ram his hips upward, but he remained where he was.

I lowered myself down slowly, sucking in first just the tip, and then, inch by inch, the rest of his thickness. There was a long groan, and I realized it was me. I loved the way he filled me, stretching and expanding my channel to accommodate his considerable girth.

William bit down on his lip, hard. "I don't know if I can stop myself. I want to flip you over and drive myself into you."

"You want faster?" I teased, giving him a smirk. "I can do faster."

I raised myself up until just the tip of him remained inside, and then slammed down hard, his balls slapping against my ass.

He growled, clutching at my hips. "Again."

I was nothing if not obliging. I gave another pump of my hips. I wasn't going to last long, and he knew it. I had a suspicion that he was barely holding on to his own orgasm. I could feel my core muscles quivering with anticipation of the impending explosion. I increased my pace, fast, faster still, until I was riding William hard. Sweat prickled at my skin, and our breaths came out in pants, gasps, and moans.

"Fuck, Brandon. I love you!" William shouted, throwing his head back.

"I love you too!" I yelled out, right as I shot cum straight across his chest, all the way to his chin. He opened his mouth to catch the farthest drops. In response, he gave an upward buck of his hips and released himself into me. I felt his cock pulse inside me, and then his knot began its expansion, filling me to the brim.

I collapsed forward onto his chest, covering myself in my own ejaculation. "That was so... wow."

"Agreed." His heaving breath ruffled my hair, and the rhythm of his heart beneath my ear finally began to slow.

"So... love, huh?" I wouldn't hold him to the declaration if it had just been said in the moment, but a part of me really wanted to believe that this baby had been made from love, and that we were bringing them into a loving family.

"I meant it," he confirmed, and then urged me to look up. "I've been feeling it for a while."

"Me too," I admitted. "I think a part of me has loved you since the moment I laid eyes on you."

"Love at first sight." He gave a slow, sexy smile. "Like we were meant to be."

"Like our baby was meant to be," I added. The thought warmed every part of me, starting at my heart and extending out to my limbs.

William gave an adorable giggle. "I can't believe we're going to be dads!" He wrapped his arms tight around me and nuzzled into the crook of my neck.

Semen squelched between our chests. "Do we have time for a shower?"

"We will make time for a shower." One minute he'd been excited and beaming, and then the cold reality of our current situation came crashing down, and his smile sagged.

I had to go back to Vala's house. We couldn't go shopping for baby furniture, I couldn't even think about the recommended doctor's appointments and blood tests. Or an ultrasound! Did that mean I wouldn't get to hear my baby's heartbeat? What if there was something wrong? And it wasn't just the baby, but my future in general that was suspended in the middle of no-man's land. Hell, where would we live in the future? It wasn't like we could go house hunting.

There was still so much I didn't know.

William must have seen the panic written all over my face. Talk about a downer. "Come on," he said, sitting up and sliding himself out of my ass. "One thing at a time. Shower first."

"Yeah. Okay." Even to my own ears my voice sounded listless. I came crashing down from the sex high, and I wasn't sure how far down I had left to fall.

William led me into the bathroom and helped me into the shower. I was half in a daze, unsure of where to begin to solve even one of my problems. William tilted my head back into the warm spray from the shower and his fingers massaged my scalp, working in the shampoo. Without a word, he soaped up my body, rinsed me clean, and then led me out and gently patted me dry with a towel.

I followed William back toward the bed and obediently stepped into the pant legs when he tapped one leg, then the other. He threaded my arms through the sleeves of the shirt. I looked up at his sullen expression as he did up the buttons for me.

"I need to wrap this up quick," I stated bluntly. "This baby needs me home... with you."

William tried to smile, but it didn't reach his eyes. "I'll be waiting for you. Whatever you need, I'm here."

Leaving his side was the hardest thing I'd ever had to do. The distance across Vala's lawn felt like ten miles, then back through the window. I placed the clothes back where I found them and shifted back into my animal, replacing the fake tooth where it belonged.

I tried to stay resolved, focus on the steps I could take to get back to William, but the reality of my situation pressed hard against my shoulders, the weight of it almost too much to bear.

What the hell was I going to do?

Days passed... nothing.

Weeks were a blur... and still nothing.

Months? Yep, you guessed it. Nada.

Shit.

Sleeping and eating were a thing of the past. My nerves were frayed to their last thread. I was just barely hanging on to my sanity.

Agent Strait paced my motel room. He'd stopped by to see me, hoping that I had more information than the FBI. Seriously.

"What the hell is he doing over there?" he snapped. "Lounging by the pool?"

"He's trying!" I snapped. I wasn't in the mood to deal with Strait's shitty attitude. "He'll get the evidence."

The agent turned to me, his eyes finally taking in my rumpled clothes, my haggard body. "Geez, what's wrong with you?"

I dropped my face into my hands. My voice came out muffled when I did my best to explain. "I just want him to come home."

We'd opted not to tell Strait about the pregnancy. Well, Brandon decided it, and I went along with his plan, against my better judgment. I was so mad at myself, and at Brandon. I understood that putting Vala away was important to him, but there had to be a limit. He was quickly approaching his due date. At first, as he started to show, he'd hidden his bump from the agents with baggy clothes, but as his waistline expanded, he'd been giving his reports over the microphone. He used the excuse that he didn't want to risk being seen sneaking out.

I thought it strange that Strait was buying into the excuse, but he was staring at me now with a scrutinizing eye. "No, there's more going on. You've both been acting strangely. I thought maybe you two had a fight and he didn't want to see you, but there's something else. What aren't you telling me?"

I buttoned my lips up tight, but as the silence stretched between us, the pressure doubled, like water behind a dam. It was too obvious that Strait was going to wait me out, no matter how long it took for me to spill the beans.

I opened my mouth to make up some excuse, but instead, the words poured out. There was no way I could stop them. "Brandon's pregnant. He's due really soon, and I don't know what to do. I didn't want him to go back to Vala's, but he's so damned stubborn." I slapped a hand across my mouth. Oops. I shouldn't have said that.

Strait's eyes widened to an almost comical bulge. His jaw wagged, like he was talking, but no sound was coming out. Finally, he at least managed to sputter. "What—he—it's—"

He shook his head and clenched his fists. "We need to get him out of there." It was nice to know that there was a rational bone in Strait's body, at least. I had half suspected that he would be willing to sacrifice my child in his single-minded focus on convicting Vala.

Strait marched out the door, and I found myself scrambling to catch up. "Where are we going?" I asked.

"Headquarters," he threw over his shoulder. "We need to extract him. Tonight, as soon as everyone goes to bed. We'll have to find another way to get that evidence." He stopped before getting into his car. "What are the chances that you have another sloth shifter on retainer?"

I shook my head sharply. "Don't you think that would be the first thing I thought of? I've searched everywhere for someone who could take his place, but none of the shifters I found would be a believable replacement. The size was wrong, or they were females and missing the speculum back patch. We had a two-toed sloth that was close, but their facial patterns are entirely wrong."

Strait looked slightly goggled at the details of a sloth's appearance. They weren't so interchangeable as he thought. "Okay. Just asking..." He disappeared into the car, and I slid into the passenger seat.

"Maybe we could make it look like the sloth escaped out a window or something," he said, spitballing ideas out loud. "Just until the baby is born. And then we can have him turn up, like, a neighbor finds him in their tree or something, and they can return him to Vala. Maybe even get a reward."

Rage tore at me. "And what? You'll just keep a father away from his newborn baby? What the hell is wrong with you?!"

His lips thinned and a blush rose on his cheeks. "You're right. I'm sorry."

I was surprised to hear an apology from him. I could tell that it was difficult for him to let this go. Their investigation had been going on for years. They'd never been able to get anything to stick to Leo Vala, and it was no doubt grating on Agent Strait.

But... when it came right down to it, he would just have to let this one go. It wasn't worth the risk. Not for Brandon, and not for our child. I would do whatever it took to keep my family safe, even if that meant making Brandon angry with me for taking away his chance at revenge. I would storm Vala's compound myself, if I had to. I would march through that front door through a hail of gunfire.

The FBI headquarters was a flurry of activity at this time of day. Strait called a meeting and got the entire team together in a conference room. When he made the announcement of Brandon's predicament, all heads in the room turned to me. Mostly judging scowls, though a few sympathetic smiles too. Yep, they all knew it was my fault that Brandon was pregnant.

I held my head up high. I was proud to claim him as my omega, and I was just as proud to be a father... but there was a feeling of shame creeping up from my gut too. I shouldn't have allowed Brandon to push his undercover role for this long. Or at all. He should've been by my side this whole time.

"All right, people, let's move out," Strait said. I hadn't been listening to his words. As long as his plan involved bringing Brandon home to me, that was all that mattered. The method was moot.

I followed along behind Strait in a daze. Down the elevator to the parking garage, and then we piled into another van, this time for a phone company. I crouched down on my seat, my entire body a mess of nerves.

We found ourselves parked down the street from Vala's place. Dusk was just beginning to fall, the sky a rosy pink. Under normal circumstances, it would be really beautiful, but now, nothing mattered except getting Brandon back in my arms. Nothing else mattered.

"We'll just wait until dark," Agent Strait assured me, patting my knee. "Soon."

I startled at the contact and darted my eyes up to meet his. "Yeah. Sure. Soon."

Soon wasn't soon enough.

FIFTEEN

BRANDON

Life as a sloth was pretty boring. Eat, sleep, poop—don't even get me started on how demoralizing it was to hang above my own feces before someone would finally decide to clean it up. Ugh. But that was only during the day. That was what Lily saw, what Leo Vala saw. Once night descended, my life was anything but boring.

In the cover of darkness, I would unlatch my cage and wander the house, looking for evidence against Big Daddy Vala. Most of his business was conducted in his personal office, and the door was usually locked, but I still tried to knob every night. Leo kept the key on him, so it wasn't like I could sneak in... and quite honestly, the FBI should've sent someone who had the skills to pick the damn lock. This was all their fault, if you looked at it like that. They didn't even bother to train me before sending me undercover.

As the sun set every night, I could feel myself tense up. Any day, I could stumble on that magic piece of evidence, and then I could go home to William. I missed him so fiercely it hurt, like a gaping hole in my chest.

Tonight, though, something was different. It took me a moment to figure out what it was. Lily was gone. Why wasn't she here? Had something happened to her?

The sun was sinking toward the horizon, painting the entire room in a rosy haze, but still, she didn't appear. It was odd not to see Lily for a long period of time like this. I was essentially her only friend, and I knew she wouldn't stay away this long if there wasn't something wrong.

I thought I could hear voices somewhere deep in the house. Was that shouting?

I needed to take a risk. My due date was getting dangerously close, and if I didn't find something soon, I would miss my chance. I slipped a claw through the bars and unhooked the latch. If I remained in my sloth form, I could wander the house in disguise, and if someone happened to see me, they would assume I'd gotten out of my cage, and no one would be the wiser.

I lowered myself down to the floor. My pregnant belly was barely noticeable as a sloth, hidden under fur and a bulbous body. As a human, though, I was as big as a house. I had been making trips to the kitchen as part of my nightly routine, filling up on as many vegetables as I could. I'd also found a container of vitamins in the medicine cupboard, so I had been supplementing wherever I could. Had to keep my iron up.

It didn't seem to matter what form I took when pulling myself across the floor. It was uncomfortable, even as a sloth. It rubbed and pulled at my muscles, causing tight spasms in my back.

As I crept down the hallway, the voices became louder, more distinct. I recognized them as Leo and his second-in command, "Uncle Bobby."

"Please," Bobby pleaded. "Please don't." Well, that didn't bode well. Begging was a sure sign that something bad was going down.

I tugged myself forward until I could peek around the corner into the living room. Uhh, was that a plastic tarp on the floor?

"Why did you do it, Bobby? Why did you steal from me?" Leo said, standing above Bobby's kneeling form. Leo's arms were crossed over his chest, straining his jacket across his broad shoulders. Just as well that he then took the jacket off and draped it over a chair. He began to roll up the sleeves of his shirt.

Bobby was watching Leo's actions with wide, fearful eyes. He shook his head frantically, his slicked hair flopping down into his face. "I didn't do it! Whoever told you that, they're lying!"

"See, I don't think they are. I looked into their claims, and it turns out... there's evidence that leads straight back to you. You took money from me, Bobby. That's like taking food straight out of my daughter's mouth."

"Lily!" Bobby yelped, latching onto her name. "Think about Lily! She's like family to me. It would break her heart if anything happened to me."

Vala shrugged. "She's young. She'll forget all about you soon enough."

"But—" Bobby was at a loss for words. Even I could see the guilt written on his face; he'd broken Leo's cardinal rule. And he would pay the ultimate price.

Watching as Leo pulled a gun from his waistband, an icy chill crept over me. I felt like I was back in time, witnessing my own father's demise. Was this how Leo had done it? Made my father kneel before him? Made him beg for his life? A sob lodged in my throat.

"Please," Bobby whispered once more, but there was no conviction behind the word. He knew his fate was sealed.

Leo raised the gun and pressed it against Bobby's forehead. "Goodbye, Bobby." And just like that, it was over. The suppressed pistol gave a pop, still startlingly loud in the enclosed space. I closed my eyes tight, but it was too late. I'd seen too much.

My grief and anguish came at me from all sides, a tidal wave of emotion. They collided inside me, low in my gut, and a searing pain tore at me. I opened my mouth and let out a high-pitched wail. I heard footsteps running toward me, and when I opened my eyes, I saw Leo Vala standing above me.

"How did you get out?" he asked.

If only it had stopped there. If only he had picked me up and put me back in my cage, I would have all the evidence I needed to get him convicted on first-degree murder. Cut and dry, open and shut. They could lock him up and throw away the key.

Except that wasn't where it ended...

The pain ripped through me again. The baby!

I curled in on myself, as if I could protect myself from the sharp edges of agony tearing me apart, but when my hands wrapped over my stomach, it was with the touch of flesh... not of fur.

I was in labor, and my body had forced me to shift back to my human form.

"What the hell?" Vala's jaw hung loose and his eyes were buggy. He'd obviously never seen a shifter before, but that didn't stop him from raising his gun to point at me. "What are you?"

I had to hope that his shock and confusion were enough to stall him from pulling that trigger. At least, long enough for help to arrive.

SIXTEEN

WILLIAM

Gods, no.

This was like some kind of nightmare, where I was trying to run but my limbs were moving in slow motion. I might as well have been running through quicksand.

We heard it all. The microphone worked as planned, and we heard the whole execution, right down to the pop of the gun, the wet splatter of blood, the thud as the body hit the floor.

I didn't stick around to hear what happened next. I pulled the van's door open, and I headed straight for Vala's front door. I didn't have a plan. Nothing beyond saving my omega, even if that meant throwing myself in front of a bullet.

I was vaguely aware of the van ripping down the street behind me. Shouting voices. Slamming doors.

The front gate was open, and I was suddenly down the driveway, up the steps, at the front door. My hand was on the knob, but of course it was locked. As much as I wanted to believe I could barge through the solid wood, my shoulder simply slammed painfully against it, and the door remained stubbornly intact.

"Out of the way!" Strait shouted behind me.

I stepped aside, even though every part of my being was screaming for me to *go go go*. A crew of agents stepped forward, wearing their bulletproof vests and helmets. I heard more vehicles screeching to a halt out front. They were all being too loud! If Vala knew we were coming, what lengths would he go to cover up the evidence... to eliminate the witnesses?

The agents had a battering ram. With a heave-ho, the sound of splintering wood rent the air. The broken door was quickly pushed aside, and the agents poured into the hallway beyond.

I made to follow them, but Strait held me back with a hand on my chest. "Let them do their job."

I gave a primal growl, and if I didn't know any better, I would say I was the one who was half animal, not Brandon. There were bangs and shouts. I dug my fingernails so hard into my palms that they drew blood. Brandon was in there. Our baby! I saw red. If anyone hurt a hair on my omega's head, there would be hell to pay.

It felt like an eternity passed before I heard a voice call, "Clear!" I shoved past Strait and dashed into the house.

The agents were everywhere. I darted my head left and right, looking for any sign of Brandon. I passed through the living room, saw the blood, the body... but there was only one body, and it wasn't Brandon. No time to process more than that.

I headed to the hall beyond, but my path was blocked by a pair of agents walking past, marching Vala between them. His arms were cuffed behind his back. I would expect him to be angry, spitting swears at the agents, but one look at his face told me he was terrified.

He was shaking his head. "One minute he was a sloth... then poof! A human! Impossible..." His incoherent blubbering trailed out the door. If you didn't know about shifters, you would think he was a raving lunatic. But as it was...

"Brandon?" I shouted, panic driving me forward. What happened? Why would he shift in front of Vala, and what did the mobster do when he realized that Lily's pet sloth was spying on him? "Brandon!"

"Here." I heard a soft groan, and when I rounded the corner, I found Brandon lying on the floor, curled into a ball. He was naked, but someone had at least thrown a jacket over him.

Brandon held his hand out to me, and I collapsed onto my knees on the floor beside him. "Where are you hurt? Did he shoot you?"

He shook his head weakly, and I ran my hands over him to make sure there was no blood. "Not shot," he mumbled, and then he gritted his teeth, his face crumpled from pain. "It's the baby. They're coming."

"Now?" I gasped. "But it's not time yet."

"Try telling that to our little one." He tried for a smile, but his face had a sickly pallor, a faint sheen of sweat beading on his brow.

A hand landed on my shoulder, and I looked up to see Strait's face, surprisingly sympathetic. "The paramedics will be here in two minutes."

Everything was happening too fast. I felt so helpless. Panic was fluttering in my chest, twisting my gut, choking my breath from my lungs. Brandon squeezed my hand, bringing my attention to him.

"You need to find Lily," he said. "She wasn't here, and I have no idea where she is. She needs us."

"Right. Lily." I turned my head up and directed my attention to the nearest agent, a woman with sharp features and a severe bun. "The little girl who lives here. She's missing." I wasn't anyone's boss—heck, I didn't even belong here in any real capacity—but there must've been something in my voice that demanded action. The agent gave a nod and jogged off to search.

The paramedics arrived, wheeling a stretcher in through the living room. They lowered it down to the floor next to Brandon and gently transferred him over. "Close your eyes, love," I whispered to him. "You don't need to look."

We were almost to the ambulance when the agent returned. "We found the girl in the kitchen with the staff," she said. "She's confused but unharmed.

A look of peace settled onto Brandon's face. "Thank gods. Please, that little girl is very important to me. Take care of her."

The woman's angular face softened. "I'll bring her to the hospital."

He sagged back onto the stretcher. "Thank you."

I climbed into the ambulance with the stretcher, and the doors slammed behind us. The engine rumbled and the ambulance pulled forward, and I felt like this was more than just driving away. This was leaving something behind. All of the grief from Brandon's past was drifting away—the guilt, the anger, the hurt from not being able to avenge his father's death.

Ahead of us lay the hospital, but also a brighter future. Brandon and I looked deeply into each other's eyes. We could do this. We could do anything, as long as we were together.

SEVENTEEN
BRANDON

I HAD NO DOUBT THAT THE AMBULANCE HAD THE best shocks that money could be, but even still, every single bump and jostle felt like we were launching into the air, smashing down against the pavement and sending a jolt of pain through me. I wanted nothing more than to descend into the warm cocoon of unconsciousness, but this baby needed me here.

I tried not to be concerned about the fact that there had been no blood tests, no ultrasounds. Guilt scrabbled at my insides. I had allowed my need for revenge to cloud my judgment.

"I'm so sorry," I said, squeezing William's hand in mine.

"Whatever for?" He was trying his best to stay positive for me, a tight smile on his lips, but there was a crease between his eyebrows, just a tiny hint of how anxious he must be.

I shook my head and winced as yet another contraction rolled through me. I breathed through it with barely a groan, and then blew out a long sigh. "I should've let it all go, left the past where it belonged. I just... couldn't see the future with my father's death still looming so large."

William leaned down and placed a kiss on my forehead, then another on my lips. "Oh, Brandon, you have no need to apologize. I understand. The future is still there for us, you know. Vala's going to go to prison for a long time. Your father's soul can rest easy."

Tears pricked at the corners of my eyes. "I wish he could've been here today. He would've been so excited to meet his grandchild."

"He's watching. I can feel it." William's smile melted into something more genuine, warmer, and it melted some of the icy fear that was threatening to take over.

It was a good thing we came by ambulance, because these contractions were practically right on top of each other. My belly felt so heavy, and there was a weight pressing down, as if my body was telling me to push.

They unloaded the gurney from the ambulance, but I gestured for them to hurry up.

"The baby's coming," I said through gritted teeth. I resisted the urge to push. You know, since I was still wearing pants and all, but also because I had zero intention of having this baby right here in the waiting room.

The nurse at the desk waggled a clipboard at us, and William got a panicked look on his face. Didn't she realize that there was no time for paperwork?

"It's okay, I've got it," Agent Strait said, jogging in through the door behind us. Lily and the severe-looking agent trailed in after him, and I wanted nothing more than to pull the little girl into my arms and tell her everything would be okay. I had to remind myself, however, that Lily wouldn't recognize me. Her fearful eyes locked with mine, and I tried to offer her a kind smile. There would be time to explain everything later.

Right now, I had a baby to deliver.

Strait grabbed the clipboard and William offered him a nod. "Thank you," he said earnestly.

As much as I had originally detested that man, I had to admit that he was starting to grow on me. Maybe he had a soft spot after all. We left him there with pen in hand, while we were whisked off down the hall and up a painfully slow elevator to a delivery room.

They quickly got me undressed and into a gown, before laying me down on a bed and raising my legs up into the stirrups. The doctor on call gave a chuckle as he took a peek. Seriously, no one wanted to have a doctor look down there and laugh.

I was about to get offended, when he said, "It's a good thing you got here when you did. This baby is ready."

"I don't need you to tell me that," I moaned. "Just tell me that I can push now!"

"Yes, by all means. Push away." His soft laugh was quickly drowned out by my roar, and I bore down.

I felt like I was being torn in two, a searing line of fire ripping straight down the middle. My baby... they were right there, on the cusp of being born. I could feel them.

"You can do it," William said in my ear. "I've got you."

And he did. His grip on my hand was like an anchor in the sea of pain I was floating through. He grounded me in a way I had never felt before. Ever since my father's death, I'd been untethered, never feeling at home in my own life. But William... he was my home now.

William... and our baby.

I clenched my jaw tight, focused my mind on the task at hand, and pushed—harder and longer than I would have thought possible. The pain, which I had been so convinced couldn't get worse... got worse! I welcomed the pain, I relished it. This was the price to pay for my baby, and I would pay it gladly.

With a final surge, I felt the baby slide from my body, and I collapsed back on the bed. The worst had passed.

"Congratulations," the doctor said. "It's a boy!"

"A boy!" William burst out, tears streaming down his cheeks. "We have a son! You did it," he whispered in my ear.

"Is he okay?" I gripped the sheets in my fists. "Please, tell me my baby is okay." I would never forgive myself if anything was wrong. I should've left sooner. Hell, I shouldn't have gone in the first place!

I held my breath as the doctor looked him over. "Ten fingers, ten toes. He looks just perfect," the doctor said.

I blew out a breath of relief. William rested his forehead on mine, and for just a moment, we shared a breath, a beat of our hearts, in perfect symmetry.

When the baby was cleaned and swaddled, a nurse brought him back to rest against my chest. The doctor and team of nurses puttered around, cleaning and stitching me up. I was only dimly aware of their bustle; I only had eyes for my son.

I must have dozed off, because the next thing I knew, I was waking up to a gentle knock on the door. "Are you up for some visitors?"

Agent Strait stuck his head in the door, and I was about to tell him to fuck off, when a second head ducked in. "Lily!" I gasped.

Strait gave a shrug. "She asked if she could see you... I figured you wouldn't mind."

"Not at all." I gestured for the little girl to come closer. "Did you want to meet the baby?"

I wasn't at all sure what kind of explanation to give her. How much could she handle? It had already been a long day, with her father's arrest. She'd lost her family and her home all in one fell swoop. Was she at all prepared to learn that her pet sloth wasn't actually a sloth?

Lily gave a hesitant nod and crept closer, peeking in at the bundle. She gave a tiny smile. "Can I hold him?" she asked in a small voice.

I thought of how tightly she had squeezed me, but William answered for me. "Do you think you can be gentle?" She nodded vigorously. "Okay, then come sit down here."

William set her up with the baby, and I watched as she sat statue-still, gazing down at the baby.

"What do you think we should name him?" I asked her.

"Lawrence," she said without a single moment of hesitation. "Booboo for short." Her eyes were dancing with joy when she looked up at me.

I laughed. Maybe explaining the whole sloth situation would be easier than I thought.

EIGHTEEN

WILLIAM

"ARE YOU SURE YOU'RE READY FOR THIS?" I asked. I knew this wasn't something he wanted to do. He *needed* to do it. And I understood that better than most.

There was a shadow of doubt in Brandon's eyes. He was the most remarkable omega I'd ever met. My instincts were screaming for me to take him far away from here, to protect him, shield him from anything even slightly negative. Instead, though, I was standing here by his side, right where I belonged.

"I'm sure." He nodded and did his best to look confident.

We walked up the steps to the FBI headquarters together, hand in hand. There was the same flurry of scurrying agents, but instead of focusing on Vala, they had moved on to new bad guys to catch, new crimes to foil

The case of Leo "Big Daddy" Vala was officially closed.

Agent Strait had done everything he could to speed up Vala's court date. We wanted him behind bars. No, not just bars, but walls too—extra thick ones. Brandon stood up in court and gave his eyewitness account... though he left off the part about how he was a sloth at the time. When it was Vala's turn on the stand, he ranted and raved about the sloth man, but in doing so, he neglected to deny any of the charges.

I'd overheard his lawyers urging him to consider an insanity plea, but he's hissed, "I'm not crazy! It really happened!"

The conviction was swift.

Vala wasn't the only one who faced a lengthy prison sentence. Several of his associates were also being put away, and Brandon went out of his way to ensure that the exotic pet dealer was punished too. No animals deserved to be mistreated, and Brandon did his part to put an end to the trade.

Today was the day Vala would be taken to prison. This was it. The end. Brandon, however, wasn't quite finished with Leo yet.

We met Strait at his office. "You ready?" he asked, looking up from his desk.

"As I'll ever be."

We were led to a small room where Vala was cuffed to a table. When Brandon walked into the room, Leo's eyes widened and he jerked back on the cuffs as if he intended to bolt. "Don't leave me alone with him!" he wailed.

"Don't worry, this'll just take a minute." Brandon looked down at his feet and wrapped his arms around his waist. "Do you remember Seth Mills?" he asked.

Vala was leaning back as far as he could in his chair, but at the mention of the name, the haze across his eyes seemed to clear. "Seth Mills?" His mouth tested the name a second time. "Yes... he—" He pressed his lips together.

Brandon looked about ready to launch himself across the table, grab Vala by the standard-issue orange jumpsuit, and shake him until something rattled loose. Instead, however, he uncurled his arms and rested his hands on the table. As he leaned forward, Vala's whole body was wracked with tremors, retreating back as far as the cuffs would allow.

"Seth Mills was my father," Brandon said slowly. "You killed him. And now I've made sure you're going to pay for it." The two men locked eyes for a long, heated moment, then Brandon turned on his heel and walked out of the room, head held high.

Leo Vala would never see a courtroom to convict him of that particular crime, but it was enough for Brandon to know that he would never be free again. Between murdering Bobby, and all of the embezzle-ment and drug trafficking, there'd been enough evidence to lock him up for life.

We walked straight out of the building and into the sunshine. Brandon turned his face up to the sky and let out a soft cry. When he looked back down, his face was wet with tears.

"Are you okay?" I asked.

He stepped into my waiting arms and took the comfort I was offering. I felt him nod against my chest.

I tipped his head back and gave him a gentle kiss. "Are you actually okay?"

He laughed softly. "Yeah. It's time, you know? I'm ready to start my life for real. And not a single part of me belongs to Vala, not anymore."

"I'm so proud of you." I lowered my lips to his once more and allowed the kiss to deepen.

"Ewww," a small voice said. It was followed by a fake barfing sound.

We looked down at Lily, and she flashed a grin back up at us. "I'm kidding. You can kiss if you want. Because you're in love, right? And people who are in love kiss."

"You are correct," William said, bopping her nose. "And you know who else I love?"

"Is it me?" she giggled.

"How did you guess?"

"You tell me all the time!" While she rolled her eyes, I could see how much she craved this love and attention. She deserved every bit of it, too.

"Are you ready to go home?" Brandon asked.

"Yep." She skipped off toward the car.

We'd asked Lily if she wanted to say goodbye to her father, but she seemed just as ready to start a new life as Brandon was. She would no doubt have to come to grips with everything that had happened sooner or later, but for now, she'd been happy enough waiting outside with our babysitter, Brandon's old boss from Fat Pizza.

"Thanks, Pop," I said, taking the baby from the large man.

"Of course," he said with a shrug. "It's always my pleasure to spend time with the kids." Pop had become a de facto grandfather to the kids, and I loved this new little family we were building. It warmed me right down to my core. We might not all be blood-related, but some family bonds were stronger than that.

Pop, not having any children of his own, needed someone to pass the restaurant to. He was getting close to retirement, and he said he would like nothing more than for Brandon to take over. Brandon, for his part, was just excited to get back to work as a waiter. He was slowly warming up to the idea of being an owner, though.

And then there was our new daughter… Lily was just the sweetest girl who ever lived, and I was beyond excited to have her officially join our family. We'd filed the paperwork this morning, and Agent Strait assured us that we wouldn't find any barriers in our way. Lily belonged with us, surrounded by love and happiness for the rest of forever.

There would be plenty more where that came from, I promised myself. More love, more kids, more life to live.

All we had to do was reach out and claim it.

EPILOGUE

BRANDON

"HURRY UP AND STICK IT IN!" I PANTED.

Oh, and that was exactly what he did. His thick cock slammed into me from behind, pressing my palms against the wall. I braced myself for the pummeling of a lifetime.

We didn't even bother taking off our shirts, there was no time! William's pants were pooled around his feet on the floor, and mine were still hooked around one ankle. Every time he thrust into me, his belt buckle gave a rattle. It was fast and furious.

"Fuck!" I cried out, my cock bouncing and my balls tightening. It had been too long. Sneaking in a quickie while the baby was napping was the best we could do.

"Shhh," he hissed.

"Harder!" I commanded, ignoring his shushing. I needed a good fuck, and he was gonna give it to me.

In response, William clutched my hips and picked up the pace. It was a good thing he was holding onto me, or I might have fallen forward onto the floor.

"Hurry," he moaned. "I'm about to come."

Knowing he was on the verge of orgasm was enough to send me hurtling toward my own climax. "William!" I shouted. I shot my load across the floor and wall.

My ass clenched tight around William's dick, and he gave a guttural bellow, which he muffled into my shoulder. With a final thrust, he spilled his seed into me, quickly followed by his knot growing and joining us together.

My legs wobbled, and my arms ached from propping myself up. "Well, this isn't exactly the best position to be stuck in. I'm kind of regretting not making an attempt at getting to the bed."

"Time was precious. I didn't want to risk us getting cut short."

Speaking of short, we heard the rumble of the school bus outside.

I looked over my shoulder at William, and he gave me a sheepish shrug. Gods, this was not the part of sex I wanted to rush.

I gave a long groan as I tugged myself forward, forcing William's knot from my channel before it was entirely ready. It was enough to give me a semi, the sheer pleasurable stretch of it.

We quickly pulled up pants and smoothed our tousled hair. There was nothing we could do about the rosy cheeks, but hopefully she wouldn't notice. We were dashing down the stairs when we heard Lawrence through the baby monitor, starting to fuss.

"No!" I whined, slapping a hand across my face. "He just went down for a nap! He can't be ready to wake up already."

"He probably heard the school bus. I'll get him," William offered.

I finished the race down the stairs to pose casually in the kitchen, just in time for Lily to walk in.

"Hey, sweetie, how was school?" I asked her. Was it just me or was my voice super high? I sounded guilty.

She didn't seem to notice, just smiled that wide, beaming grin. "It was so good! There was a visitor from the zoo! He brought a bunch of animals, and one of them was a sloth."

William joined us, carrying Lawrence. The baby wasn't so much of a baby anymore. He broke into a massive, chubby smile as soon as he saw Lily, showing off those dimples of his. He held out his arms, making grabby hands for her.

"Booboo!" She giggled and swooped forward to cuddle him. They got settled in at the kitchen table to have a long chat... which was basically just Lily talking and Lawrence giving her his undivided attention. He was a very good listener.

William went over to the fridge to pull out the makings of an after-school snack. "I can't believe we got away with that," he whispered to me.

"It was close," I muttered under my breath. "But it was also—"

"Super hot," he finished for me.

"Yeah, that."

We were silent for a moment while he put together a sandwich. Then he leaned over and asked, "Can we do it again later?"

"If you don't mind," I teased.

"If I must." He gave an exaggerated sigh. "An alpha's work is never done."

"Uh, Dads?" Lily interrupted.

We looked over to where she was sitting with Lawrence, but instead of our son, in his place was a sloth.

Lily looked excited. "I was just telling Booboo about the sloth they brought in at school, and then he just turned into one!" she squealed. "You're not mad at me, right? It's not my fault."

"Of course not," I assured her. "You didn't do anything wrong. In fact, you've actually done us a favor. We didn't know if your little brother was a shifter or not."

"Well, now we know," William said with a little nod. For a human, he was handling this all remarkably well.

"We'll have to be careful," I told Lily. "This is a secret, and you can't tell anyone."

"This is the best secret ever!" She clapped her hands. "Can I tell my best friend Sarah?"

Oh boy. William and I exchanged a look. We had our work cut out for us, but it was the best kind of work to have.

"Let's go over the meaning of secret again," William said, trying his best to hold in his laugh.